The Magic Rabbit

HATS Men's Ladies' PANTS
PIZZA + SUBS

The Magic Rabbit

Annette LeBlanc Cate

WALKER BOOKS
AND SUBSIDIARIES
LONDON • BOSTON • SYDNEY • AUCKLAND

First published 2007 by Walker Books Ltd
87 Vauxhall Walk, London SE11 5HJ

2 4 6 8 10 9 7 5 3 1

This book has been handlettered by Annette LeBlanc Cate.

Printed in China

British Library Cataloguing in Publication Data:
a catalogue record for this book is
available from the British Library

ISBN 978-1-84428-290-6

www.walkerbooks.co.uk

For Mom and Dad

HOUDINI
MYSTERIES
OF THE
EAST
PAINT
RED
SEE THE AMA

Ray and Bunny lived together in a tiny apartment in the city. They were business partners. Ray was a magician and Bunny was his loyal assistant.

They were also best friends. They did everything together.

Abracadabra…

Every Saturday Ray and Bunny took their magic show into town. But one Saturday it was a little more crowded than usual. And just as Ray said the magic word and Bunny was about to leap from the hat in a spray of glittering stars...

Oof!
CRASH!

The scene became a terrible tangle of balls and stars, juggler and magician, hat and...
"Bunny? Bunny, where are you?" shouted Ray.
The hat was empty. Bunny was gone!

Bunny wandered along the dark street, thinking of Ray and wishing that they were sitting down to dinner together right now, at their own little table in the kitchen.

All around him, people were hurrying home to their own dinners. No one stopped or even seemed to notice the lost little bunny.

Bunny hopped along a little further, then slipped down a dark alley to rest. He was tired and hungry and missed Ray terribly. A tear rolled down his nose. His nose twitched. Then... his nose twitched again. Bunny smelled something good to eat.

It was popcorn, his favourite!

Bunny got straight down to business. As he was nibbling, he noticed something shining among the kernels. Glittering stars! Lots of them!

Bunny followed the path
of stars out of the alley,

along the street...

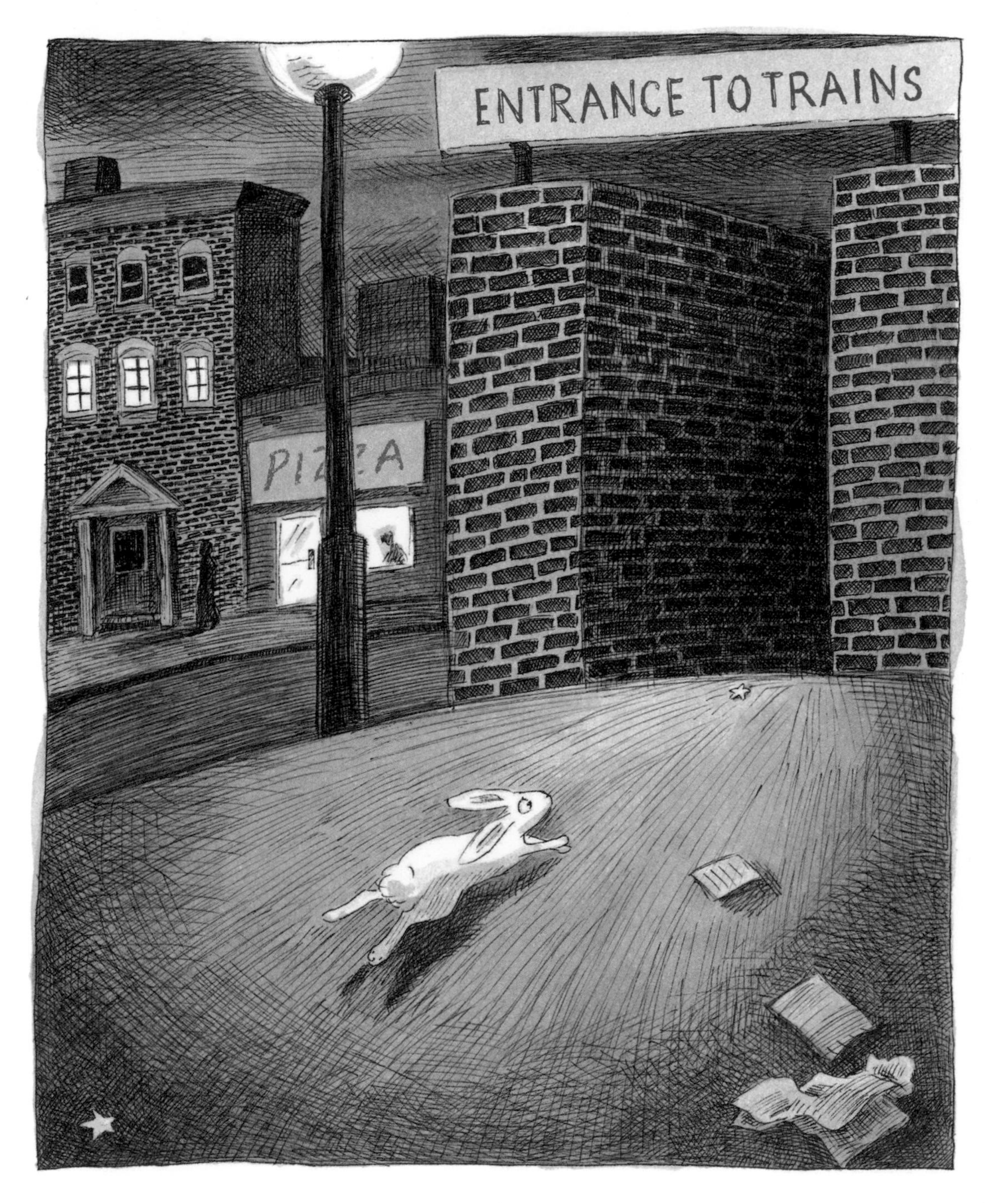

up a hill…

down some stairs…

and through the underground station, all the way to . . .

his very own hat!

The last train of the night pulled away.
Only a magician and his bunny assistant were left on the platform.
But two old friends never mind walking home together.